THIS WALKER BOOK BELONGS TO:

_____

_____

_____

_____

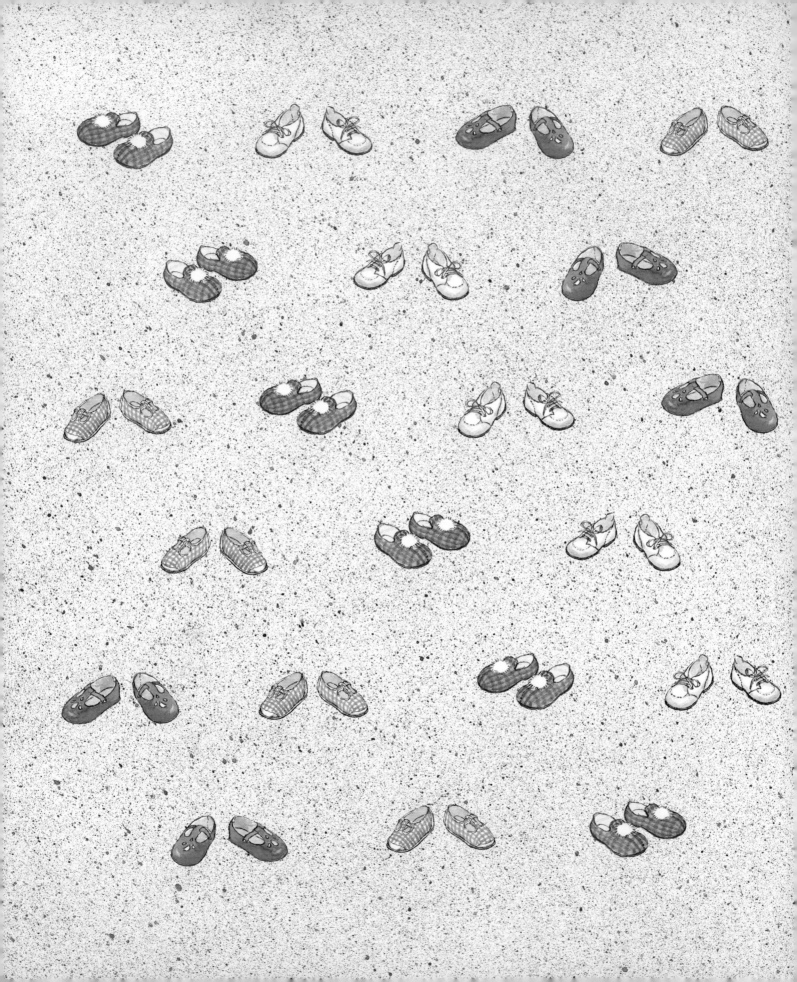

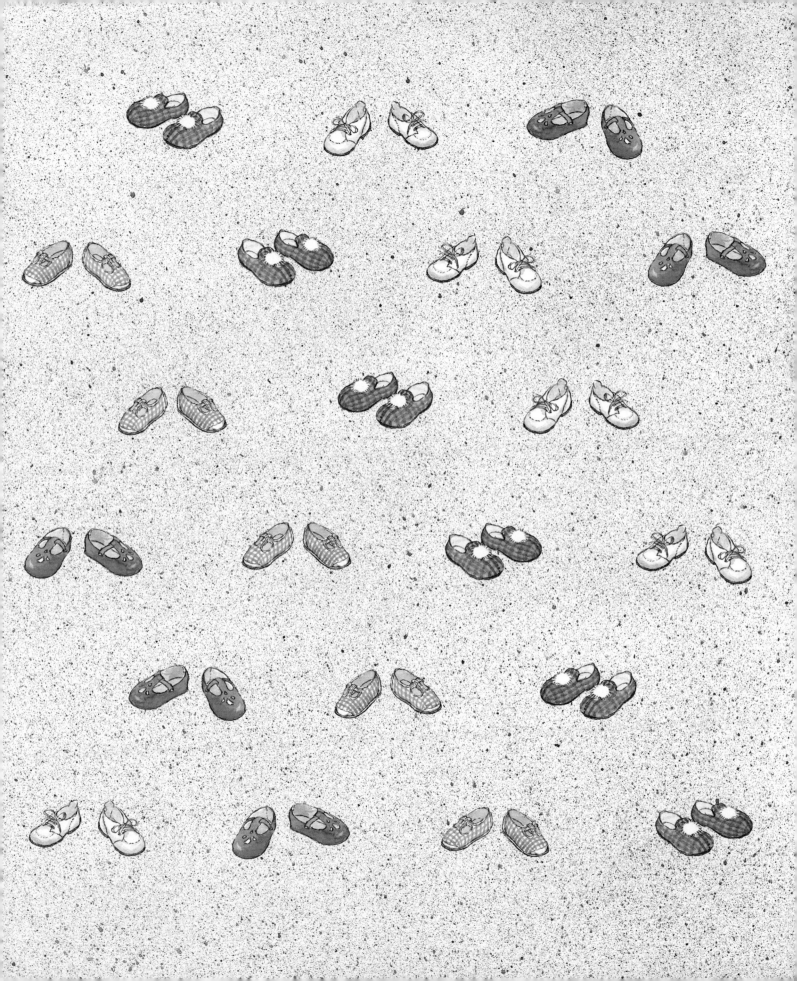

For Mara and Marissa
M.W.

For Sarah, Rowan, Rachel,
Helen, Sarah W. and Charlie…
Giants to be.
P.D.

First published 1989 by Walker Books Ltd
87 Vauxhall Walk, London SE11 5HJ

This edition published 1991

10 12 14 15 13 11 9

Text © 1989 Martin Waddell
Illustrations © 1989 Penny Dale

The right of Martin Waddell to be identified as author
of this work has been asserted by him in accordance
with the Copyright, Designs and Patents Act 1988.

Printed in Hong Kong

British Library Cataloguing in Publication Data
A catalogue record for this book is
available from the British Library.

ISBN 0-7445-1791-5

Once There Were
GIANTS

Written by Martin Waddell

Illustrated by Penny Dale

WALKER BOOKS
AND SUBSIDIARIES
LONDON · BOSTON · SYDNEY

Once there were Giants in our house.

There were Mum and Dad and
Jill and John and Uncle Tom.

The small one on the rug is me.

When I could sit up
Mum bought a high chair.
I sat at the table
way up in the sky
with Mum and Dad and
Jill and John and Uncle Tom.

The one throwing porridge is me.

When I could crawl
I crawled round the floor.
Dad was a dragon and
he gave a roar that scared
Jill and John and Uncle Tom.

The one who is crying is me.

When I could walk
I walked to the park with
Jill and John and Uncle Tom.
We fed the ducks and
Jill stood on her head.

The one in the duck pond is me.

When I could talk
I talked and talked!
I annoyed Uncle Tom and
got sat upon by Jill and by John.
That's John on my head
and Jill on my knee.

The one on my bottom is me!

When I could run
I ran and ran,
chased by Mum and Dad
and Uncle Tom and
Jill on her bike and
my brother John.

The one who is puffed out is me.

When I went to playgroup
I wouldn't play games and
I called people names and
upset the water on Millie Magee.
She's the one with the towel.

The one being scolded is me!

When I went to school
I'd got bigger by then.
Mum had to leave at
a quarter to ten and
she didn't come back
for a long, long time.
I didn't shout and
I didn't scream.
She came for me at
a quarter to three.

The one on Mum's knee is me.

When I went to the top class
I had lots of fun.
I got big and strong
and punched my brother John.
He's the one with the sore nose.

The one with the black eye is me.

When I went to Big School
I was taller than Mum,
and nearly as tall as my Uncle Tom.
But I never caught up
with my brother John.
I ran and I jumped
and they all came to see.
There they are cheering.

The one who's just winning is me.

When I went to work
I lived all by myself.

Then I met Don and we married.

There's Jill and John
and Uncle Tom
and Mum's the one crying,
and Dad is the one
with the beer on his head.

The bride looking happy is me!

Then we had a baby girl
and things changed.

There are Giants in our house again!

There is my husband, Don,

and Jill and John,

my Mum and my Dad

and Uncle Tom

and one of the Giants is…

ME!

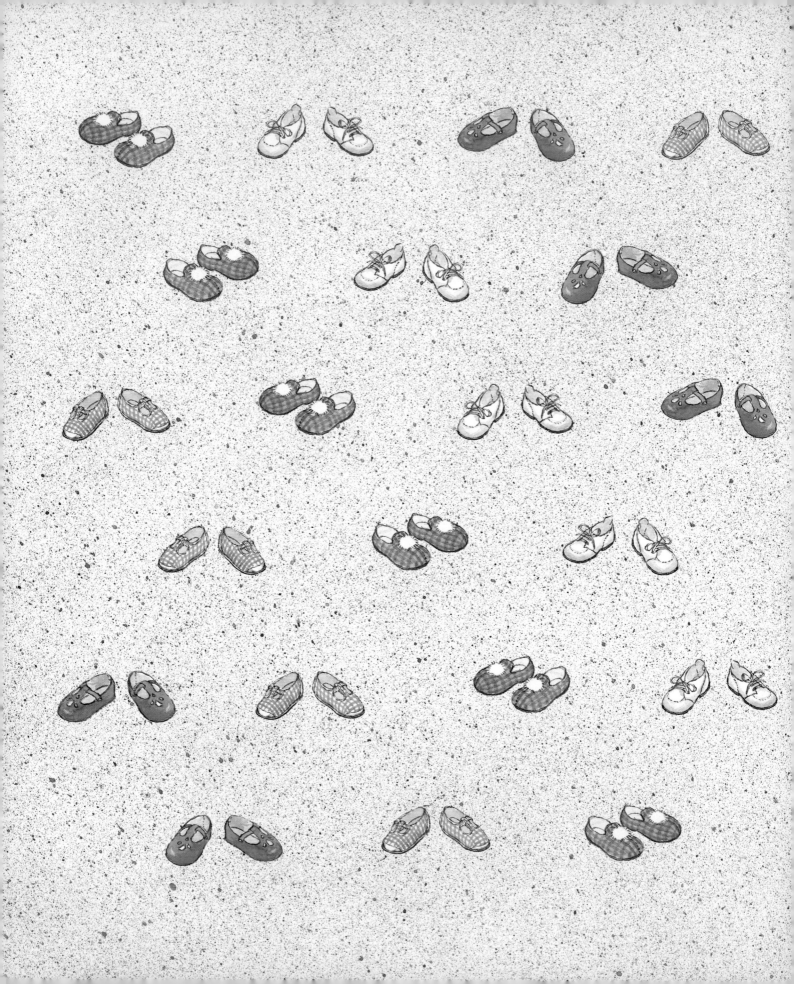

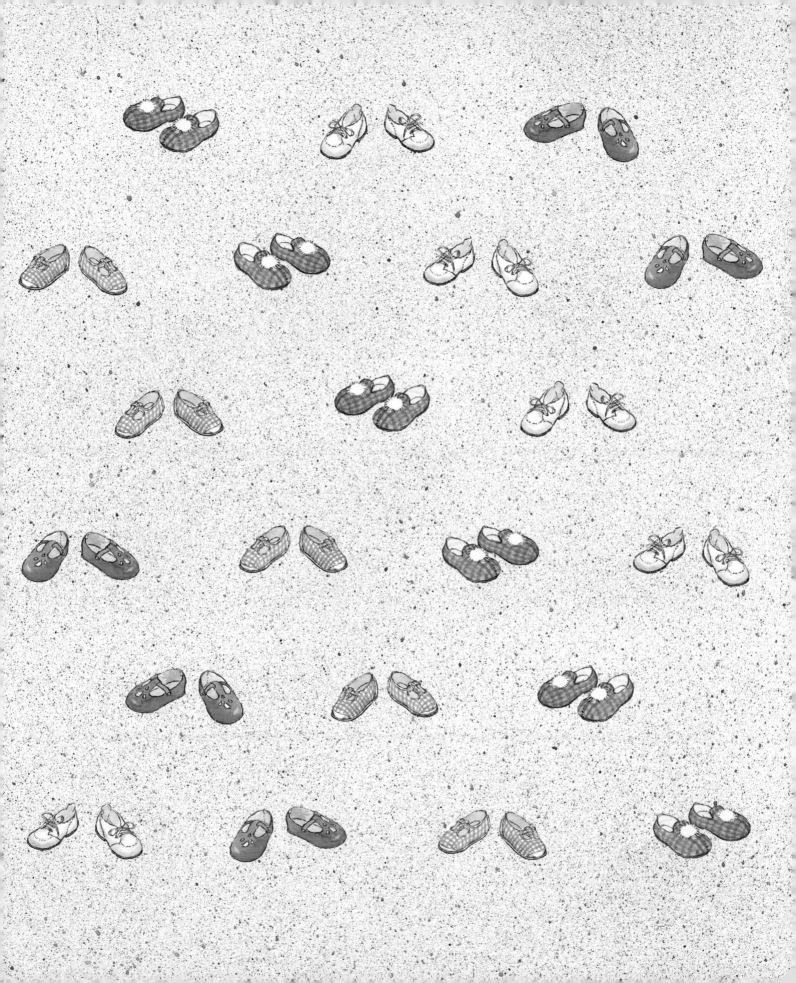

MORE WALKER PAPERBACKS
For You to Enjoy

MY GREAT GRANDPA
by Martin Waddell / Dom Mansell

A book about the very special relationship between the young and the very old.
"Charming story… Expansive, detailed pictures." *School Library Journal*
ISBN 0-7445-2011-8   £4.99

AMY SAID
by Martin Waddell / Charlotte Voake

Staying at Gran's is a riot for Amy and her brother!
"A triumph… Understatement and lightness of touch couldn't find better exposition."
John Lawrence, The Times Educational Supplement
ISBN 0-7445-5227-3   £4.99

BET YOU CAN'T!
by Penny Dale

"A lively argumentative dialogue – using simple, repetitive words –
between two children. Illustrated with great humour and realism."
Practical Parenting

ISBN 0-7445-1225-5   £4.50

WAKE UP, MR. B!
by Penny Dale

When Rosie wakes up early, only her dog, Mr. B, will play with her – and what a time they have!
"Perceptive, domestic illustrations fill a varied cartoon-strip format …
making this a lovely tell-it-yourself picture book."
The Good Books Guide
ISBN 0-7445-1467-3   £4.50